MW01265476

Inside the NBA
Minnesota Timberwolves

Paul Joseph

219 6011

ABDO & Daughters
PUBLISHING

Published by Abdo & Daughters, 4940 Viking Dr., Suite 622, Edina, MN 55435.

Copyright ©1997 by Abdo Consulting Group, Inc., Pentagon Tower, P.O. Box 36036, Minneapolis, Minnesota 55435. International copyrights reserved in all countries. No part of this book may be reproduced in any form without written permission from the publisher. Printed in the United States.

Cover photo: Allsport
Interior photos: Allsport, pages 1, 5, 15, 17, 22, 27
                Wide World Photos, pages 9, 10, 16
                Sports Illustrated, page 24

Edited by Kal Gronvall

Library of Congress Cataloging–in–Publication Data

Joseph, Paul, 1970-
    The Minnesota Timberwolves / by Paul Joseph
       p. cm. — (Inside the NBA)
    Includes index.
    Summary: Provides an overview of the history and key personalities of the expansion team that brought professional basketball back to Minnesota in 1989.
    ISBN   1-56239-765-6
    1. Minnesota Timberwolves (Basketball team)—History—Juvenile literature. [1. Minnesota Timberwolves (Basketball team)—History. 2. Basketball—History.] I. Title. II. Series.
GV885.52.M565J67   1997
796.323' 64' 09776579—dc21   96-3812
                                    CIP
                                    AC

Contents

Minnesota Timberwolves

The Minnesota Timberwolves joined the National Basketball Association (NBA) for the 1989-90 season as part of a two-phase league expansion that also brought in the Orlando Magic, Miami Heat, and Charlotte Hornets. The state of Minnesota once again enjoyed NBA play with the arrival of the Timberwolves. The former home of the Lakers, Minnesota had desperately tried for roughly three decades to get a franchise.

The Minneapolis Lakers of the early 1950s had been the dominant team of that era. Led by 6-foot, 10-inch George Mikan, the first great pro center, the Lakers won five championships in six years. Four years later, however, the Lakers moved to Los Angeles.

Since their inaugural season of 1989-90, the Timberwolves have struggled, failing to win more than 29 games in any season. All expansion teams have trouble in the beginning, but the Timberwolves had more than their share of woes. Bad luck in the lottery, terrible draft choices, even worse trades, inexperienced front-office people, and poor coaching, all led to losing seasons.

Facing page: The Timberwolves' Stephon Marbury drives the ball down the court.

But the tide has now changed for the T-Wolves. Glen Taylor took over as the new owner, and he wants nothing more than to build a championship team. His first move was to make Kevin McHale, a Minnesota native and Boston Celtic great, the vice president of basketball operations. McHale has made deals, drafted well, and has a great threesome to build around in power forward Tom Gugliotta, point guard Stephon Marbury, and all-around superstar Kevin Garnett.

Behind this threesome, the Timberwolves won the most games in their history and made the postseason for the first time in the 1996-97 season. It shouldn't be long before the Timberwolves become a true force in the NBA.

Starting An Expansion Franchise

In 1989, Minneapolis businessmen Harvey Ratner and Marv Wolfenson brought NBA basketball back to Minnesota after a 29 year layoff. Friends since boyhood, the pair had made their fortunes in real estate and in the health club business.

The Timberwolves began play in 1989, but attempts to win a franchise date back to 1984. Joining "Harv and Marv" in the quest for an NBA team in Minnesota was a task force led by ex-Laker great George Mikan.

The threesome initially made offers for the Milwaukee Bucks, San Antonio Spurs, and Utah Jazz. Those deals all fell through. But in 1987, the NBA voted to add four teams over the next two seasons. Charlotte and Miami were added for the 1988-89 season, and Orlando and Minnesota were added for 1989-90.

Harv and Marv were the principal investors in the $32 million franchise. In addition, the owners were building a state-of-the-art arena, the luxurious Target Center in downtown Minneapolis.

A regional "Name the Team" contest favored "Timberwolves" over "Polars" by a two-to-one margin. Now that the Minnesota Timberwolves were an official NBA franchise, the hard part would begin—building a team.

Musselman Named First Head Coach

On August 23, 1988, Bill Musselman was named head coach. He was known throughout the Minnesota sports community for leading the University of Minnesota to a Big Ten Conference championship in 1971-72. He also had coaching stints in the NBA with the Cleveland Cavaliers, in the American Basketball Association (ABA), and in the Continental Basketball Association (CBA), where he led his teams to four straight championships.

Now, however, Musselman had the biggest job of his career—building an NBA franchise from scratch. He would begin with the Expansion Draft, where the T-Wolves and Orlando were able to choose unprotected players from any NBA team.

Minnesota's first choice in the NBA Expansion Draft was power forward Rick Mahorn from the then-World Champion Detroit Pistons. Mahorn heard the news less than an hour after a rally celebrating the Pistons' championship, and he was furious. In the end, he never played for the T-Wolves. Instead, he was traded to the Philadelphia 76ers for several high draft picks.

Other players selected by Minnesota in the Expansion Draft included Tyrone Corbin, Steve Johnson, Brad Lohaus, David Rivers, Mark Davis, and Scott Roth.

In the college draft a week later, the Timberwolves took UCLA point guard Jerome "Pooh" Richardson with the 10th pick overall. The team also selected Villanova guard Doug West, and center Gary Leonard in later rounds.

Doug West drives past a heavy Los Angeles Lakers' defense.

T-Wolves' First Season

Musselman's 1989-90 Minnesota Timberwolves made their NBA debut on November 3, 1989, against the SuperSonics in Seattle. The starting lineup consisted of Sam Mitchell, Tod Murphy, Brad Lohaus, Tony Campbell, and Sidney Lowe. Mitchell scored the first two points in club history on a pair of free throws. Minnesota ended up losing their first game 106-94.

Sam Mitchell is fouled by Toronto Raptors' Popeye Jones.

Five days later the T-Wolves were welcomed home to their temporary arena, the Metrodome. They played their entire first season there while waiting for the Target Center to be completed. The spacious Metrodome provided excellent temporary housing for the rookie Timberwolves. So ample was the seating that at season's end, Minnesota had set a new all-time attendance record with well over a million paying customers.

In their home opener, however, Minnesota lost to Chicago, 96-84, as the Bulls' Michael Jordan scored 45 points. The Wolves finally got their first win on November 10, beating the Philadelphia 76ers 125-118 in overtime. Campbell and Corbin led the way for Minnesota hitting for 38 and 36 points.

December opened with a big 27-point win over Cleveland. Then the team hit a bad spell, losing nine in a row. Even while losing, Musselman stressed defense to his young team. Through 29 games they held opposing teams to 101.5 points per game to rank fifth in the NBA.

In January, rookie point guard Pooh Richardson moved into the starting lineup and responded with 20 points and 10 assists. After that game everyone knew that Pooh was the future of the team.

In February, the T-Wolves grabbed six wins, including a team-high four-game winning streak. Tony Campbell had the team's highest scoring game of the season when he netted 44 points against the Celtics.

Minnesota finished the season with an impressive inaugural record of 22-60, the best among the NBA's four newest teams. The Wolves ended the season ranked second in the NBA in team defense, having allowed only 99.4 points per game. Campbell led the team in scoring, averaging 23.2 points per game. Richardson was named to the NBA All-Rookie First Team. Not a bad start for the rookie Timberwolves.

Continuing To Build

The Timberwolves opened their second season in the brand-new Target Center. Before a sellout crowd of 19,006, the T-Wolves beat the Dallas Mavericks 98-85. After that opening night win, the Wolves lost many more than they won. In December, they suffered a seven-game losing streak.

In January, Musselman scrapped his controlled offense in favor of a run-and-gun style. The more wide-open approach led to a three-game road winning streak. The Wolves continued to improve, winning seven games in April, and six of their last eight of the season. One of those games was highlighted by an impressive outing of 134 points in a victory over the Denver Nuggets.

The Timberwolves finished the season with 29 victories, which is very impressive for a second year team. Tony Campbell led the Wolves in scoring with a 21.8 average.

Although the Timberwolves improved by seven games from their inaugural season and looked like a team on the rise, management decided to fire Musselman. In June, former Boston Celtic assistant coach Jimmy Rodgers was named head coach. It would not be an easy task for Rodgers.

Expansion-Club Blues

The Timberwolves had a different look when they opened their 1991-92 season. Gerald Glass and Doug West replaced veterans Corbin and Campbell in the starting lineup. Corbin was then traded to the Utah Jazz for 6-foot, 11-inch forward Thurl Bailey. The Wolves also added 7-foot, 2-inch Luc Longley, who was their seventh overall pick in the 1991 NBA Draft. Longley became the first Australian to play in the NBA.

Injuries hurt the Timberwolves as the team went from bad to worse. In December, the Wolves suffered the worst month in franchise history, winning only one game.

The T-Wolves bounced back in January, winning three of their first six games. But from there everything went downhill as Minnesota logged a 10-game losing streak. The losses kept coming. From February 29 to March 29, the Wolves lost 16 straight. The team's final record of 15-67 is still the worst in their young history.

For the Minnesota Timberwolves, the expansion blues had set in. Fans were losing interest, and for the third year in a row the lottery did not tip in the Wolves' favor. Looking toward the 1992 NBA Draft, the T-Wolves thought that they had a chance to acquire Shaquille O'Neal. But it wasn't to be. Instead they had to settle for Duke center Christian Laettner with their third overall pick.

Laettner Comes On Board

Christian Laettner was College Player of the Year and was part of the original "Dream Team," but in no way could he make the impact that O'Neal would. The 6-foot, 11-inch, 235-pound Laettner was the only player in college history to start in four Final Fours. To say that Laettner was the most talented player to wear a Wolves jersey up to this point would be an understatement. But what the Wolves were looking for was either the lottery prize, Shaquille O'Neal, or the second pick, Alonzo Mourning. Of course, with the Wolves' luck, they chose third and acquired Laettner.

Also, in 1992, Jack McCloskey was named general manger of the Wolves. For 13 years he had held that same position with the Detroit Pistons, building a team that won back-to-back championships. Throughout the NBA, McCloskey was known as "Trader Jack" because of his trade-happy ways. He pulled the trigger on 43 trades while he was with the Pistons.

McCloskey's first job was to choose Laettner in the draft, which was a no-brainer. His first real move was trading Pooh Richardson and Sam Mitchell to the Indiana Pacers for "Rifleman" Chuck Person and point guard Michael Williams.

Facing page: Christian Laettner gets set for a free throw.

The Timberwolves had a solid lineup that looked to compete. Laettner's NBA career got off to a good start as he averaged 19.5 points and 8.1 rebounds through the first month. Doug West was a skilled shooter. Williams was both a playmaker and scorer, and Person was one of the best shooters in the league.

In December, however, Minnesota won only one game. On January 11, McCloskey made a coaching change. He fired Rodgers and hired Sidney Lowe as head coach. The team improved under Lowe but still struggled.

The Wolves improved slightly from the year before, finishing the season with a 19-63 record. Laettner was selected to the NBA All-Rookie First Team. He finished the season averaging 18.2 points and 8.2 rebounds per game. The following year Laettner would get another teammate to help him with the scoring.

Chuck Person backs his way to the hoop against the Seattle SuperSonics.

J.R. Rider fights for
two underneath.

A Bumpy Ride With Rider

In the 1993 NBA Draft, the Minnesota Timberwolves acquired one of the most explosive offensive forces to ever come out of college. University of Nevada-Las Vegas star guard Isaiah "J.R." Rider averaged nearly 30 points per game his senior year in college and was expected to bring his much-needed offensive force into the Wolves' lineup.

Minnesota

Doug West has been with the Wolves since the team's formation, from 1989 to 1997.

Sam Mitchell scored the first points in Minnesota Timberwolves history in 1989.

Christian Laettner made the NBA All-Rookie First Team in 1992-93, averaging over 18 points per game.

Timberwolves

Since joining the Timberwolves in 1995, Tom Gugliotta has led the team in scoring.

Kevin Garnett was the fifth pick taken overall in the 1995 NBA Draft, coming straight from high school.

Stephon Marbury made the 1996-97 NBA All-Rookie First Team and was runner-up for the Rookie of the Year Award.

Rider's rookie year was even better than expected. He averaged 16.6 points, 4.0 rebounds, and 2.6 assists per game. For his efforts he was named to the NBA All-Rookie First Team. As he predicted when he was first drafted by the Wolves, Rider came out in All-Star Weekend on his home court at the Target Center, and easily won the Slam-Dunk Championship. Rider iced the contest in the final round when he drove down the baseline, flew through the air, whipped the ball between his legs, and slammed it home for one of the most unbelievable dunks in contest history.

Laettner continued to be a team leader on the court. He pumped in 16.8 points and grabbed 8.6 rebounds per game to lead the Timberwolves in both categories.

The Laettner-Rider combo, however, only added a one-victory improvement from the previous year. Minnesota lost five straight games to open the season, and then only managed 20 wins the rest of the way.

Even though the Wolves were experiencing a bumpy ride, attendance was still at an all-time high. But then, in a move that shocked the entire state of Minnesota, the Timberwolves were sold to a group of investors who were intending to move the franchise to New Orleans. Luckily, the NBA Board of Governors vetoed the sale. Another ownership group, led by Glen Taylor, took over. Taylor, a Minnesota native, promised to keep the Timberwolves in Minnesota and build a championship team.

Troubles Continue

Before the 1994-95 season began, Bill Blair replaced Sidney Lowe as head coach. The Wolves also drafted the talented forward Donyell Marshall from the University of Connecticut. Marshall was supposed to step in and be a solid force for the Wolves. Instead, he signed the largest contract in Timberwolves' history and then turned into a slug. To say he was lazy and unmotivated would be an understatement.

Rider also started to show his true colors and turned into a thug. If he wasn't in trouble with the law, he was in trouble with the team, missing team meetings, practices, plane rides, and games.

The turmoil hurt the team considerably. The Timberwolves set an NBA record by losing at least 60 games for the fourth consecutive season. The team finished 21-61, for last place in the Midwest Division.

When Rider wanted to, he showed flashes of the player he could be. He led the team in scoring with 20.4 points per game. Laettner stayed consistent, averaging 16.3 points per game. Laettner, however, was not happy playing in Minnesota and showed it daily with his constant whining.

The season brightened up considerably when the Wolves made the greatest trade in franchise history. Donyell Marshall was traded after only half a season with the Wolves to the Golden State Warriors for Tom Gugliotta. Gugliotta came in and made an immediate impact, averaging 14.4 points, 7.2 rebounds, and 4.5 assists. He also became a fan-favorite as chants of "Googs" were heard throughout the Target Center whenever he scored.

Two Kevins Take Over

Before the 1995-96 season began, general manager Jack McCloskey retired. Timberwolves owner Glen Taylor was determined to find someone who could evaluate talent and build a winner. Taylor found that man in Minnesota native and Boston Celtic great Kevin McHale. McHale was named vice president of basketball operations, taking over the day-to-day activities of the team.

McHale's main duties were putting together a winning combination. McHale went to work quickly, as he made a bold selection in the 1995 NBA Draft, taking high-school phenom Kevin "Da' Kid" Garnett with the fifth overall pick.

Kevin Garnett, a 6-foot, 11-inch forward, made the jump directly from high school to the NBA. Many doubted that he could make an impact in the NBA after only playing in high school. Garnett, however, soon proved his critics wrong.

After spending his first three years of high school playing for Mauldin High School in South Carolina, Garnett moved to Chicago and played for Farragut Academy. As a senior, Garnett was named National High School Player of the Year and was selected to the Parade Magazine All-America First Team. He led Farragut to a 28-2 mark and the Class AA state quarterfinals.

Facing page: Kevin Garnett flies over Luc Longley and slams the ball home.

23

Garnett easily won the Mr. Basketball-Illinois after averaging 25.2 points, 17.9 rebounds, 6.7 assists, and 6.5 blocks while shooting .666 from the field. The year before, Garnett was named Mr. Basketball-South Carolina.

Although everyone knew that Garnett had awesome basketball talent, most believed he needed to play in college first before making that step to the NBA. Kevin McHale thought otherwise. Although only a handful of players have made that leap from high school to the pros, McHale believed that Garnett had the tools necessary to be an impact player.

Garnett became that impact player. As his rookie season wore on, Garnett got better. He became a starter midway through the season and became the third-youngest player ever to start a game at 19 years, 235 days. Garnett earned All-Rookie Second Team honors after averaging 10.6 points, 6.3 rebounds, and 1.64 blocked shots.

Best of all, Garnett had fun playing. He was a welcome addition to a franchise that had seen its share of troubled players. He quickly turned into a fan-favorite by playing hard, hustling, being a team leader, and always having a smile on his face.

Tom Gugliotta shoots a fall-away under heavy pressure.

More Positive Changes

With this new attitude started by the two Kevins, the Timberwolves began to improve. The attitude improved even more when McHale let head coach Bill Blair go midway through the 1995-96 season, replacing him with Phil "Flip" Saunders.

Saunders was a college teammate of Kevin McHale at the University of Minnesota, and later an assistant coach with the Gophers. Before taking over the Wolves, Saunders was a two-time CBA Coach of the Year.

Saunders brought a winning attitude with him and knew how to get the most out of his young team. After four straight seasons of 60-plus losses, Saunders led the Wolves to a 26-56 record, the second best season in their seven-year history.

Before the season had ended, another positive change took place. Laettner, unhappy in Minnesota, and McHale, unhappy with Laettner's attitude, traded him, along with Sean Rooks, to the Atlanta Hawks for Andrew Lang and Spud Webb.

The trade paved the way for Kevin Garnett and Tom Gugliotta to become the foundation on which the Timberwolves could build a winner. More importantly, the trade helped acquire the point guard of the future, and finally give the Wolves three solid stars to build the team around.

Another Kid!

In the 1996 NBA Draft, the Minnesota Timberwolves had the fifth pick. Once again, the player they wanted would go before that. This time, however, McHale didn't sit back. The player the Wolves wanted was point-guard Stephon Marbury. Unfortunately, the Milwaukee Bucks chose Marbury with the fourth pick. McHale, determined to get his man, gave the Bucks Andrew Lang, a future draft choice, and Minnesota's number five pick, Ray Allen.

The Wolves biggest need was a point guard, and now they would be secure for many years to come with Marbury on board. Marbury, only 19 years old at the time of the draft, played only one year in college. The 6-foot, 2-inch Marbury dazzled the Atlantic Coast Conference (ACC), while playing for Georgia Tech, averaging 18.9 points per game in his only college season.

McHale knew that Marbury was the player he wanted after seeing him play in college. Marbury led his team and ranked third in the ACC in scoring. He was named third-team All-America and named ACC Rookie of the Year.

The Wolves now had two legitimate stars in Garnett and Marbury. Many called them the next John Stockton and Karl Malone, while others went as far as to call them the next Michael Jordan and Scottie Pippen. The fact is, the two of them were great friends before the draft and had hoped to someday play in the NBA together. Now that it has happened they both want to win a championship.

Garnett and Marbury had played together in high school All-Star Games and became close friends. In Garnett's rookie year and Marbury's freshman year the two would talk weekly on the phone.

Garnett got Marbury excited about the possibility of becoming a T-Wolf.

"When I found out I was going to Minnesota, a chill went down my body," said Marbury. "This is like starting a new marriage.... A dream come true in all ways."

McHale is just as excited about having "Da' Kids" on his team. "The two [Garnett and Marbury] want to become great players. You don't win championships without superstars. We feel a big gap has been filled, we have two superstars."

Kevin Garnett and Stephon Marbury.

The Best Season Ever

The Timberwolves had their best season ever in 1996-97. Behind the threesome of Garnett, Marbury, and Gugliotta the Wolves captured 40 wins and made the postseason for the first time. This talented threesome are three of the best players on the same team. Googs is the old guy at 27. Da' Kids still haven't hit 21 years old.

In the playoffs Minnesota fought hard but were taken out in the first round by the veteran Houston Rockets. The Rockets, led by Hakeem Olajuwon, Charles Barkley, and Clyde Drexler were too much for the inexperienced T-Wolves.

From the owner to the front-office, from the coaching staff to the players, this organization truly wants to build a championship team. Glen Taylor will not be happy until he sees a banner hanging from the rafters, and he is willing to spend the money to do it. Kevin McHale has turned into a mastermind in evaluating talent and making deals. And coach Flip Saunders has his team believing they can win.

The Timberwolves will continue to build around the core group. If the team can get a few more pieces to fill in around Googs and Da' Kids, it won't be long before the Timberwolves are vying for the NBA Championship.

Glossary

American Basketball Association (ABA)—A professional basketball league that rivaled the NBA from 1967 to 1976 until it merged with the NBA.

assist—A pass of the ball to the teammate scoring a field goal.

Basketball Association of America (BAA)—A professional basketball league that merged with the NBL to form the NBA.

center—A player who holds the middle position on the court.

championship—The final basketball game or series, to determine the best team.

draft—An event held where NBA teams choose amateur players to be on their team.

expansion team—A newly-formed team that joins an already established league.

fast break—A play that develops quickly down court after a defensive rebound.

field goal—When a player scores two or three points with one shot.

Finals—The championship series of the NBA playoffs.

forward—A player who is part of the front line of offense and defense.

franchise—A team that belongs to an organized league.

free throw—A privilege given a player to score one point by an unhindered throw for goal from within the free-throw circle and behind the free-throw line.

guard—Either of two players who initiate plays from the center of the court.

jump ball—To put the ball in play in the center restraining circle with a jump between two opponents at the beginning of the game, each extra period, or when two opposing players each have control of the ball.

Most Valuable Player (MVP) Award—An award given to the best player in the league, All-Star Game, or NBA Finals.

National Basketball Association (NBA)—A professional basketball league in the United States and Canada, consisting of the Eastern and Western conferences.

National Basketball League (NBL)—A professional basketball league that merged with the BAA to form the NBA.

National Collegiate Athletic Association (NCAA)—The ruling body which oversees all athletic competition at the college level.

personal foul—A player foul which involves contact with an opponent while the ball is alive or after the ball is in the possession of a player for a throw-in.

playoffs—Games played by the best teams after the regular season to determine a champion.

postseason—All the games after the regular season ends; the playoffs.

rebound—To grab and control the ball after a missed shot.

rookie—A first-year player.

Rookie of the Year Award—An award given to the best first-year player in the league.

Sixth Man Award—An award given yearly by the NBA to the best non-starting player.

trade—To exchange a player or players with another team.

Index